JADA JONES

★ CLASS ACT ★

JADA JONES

★ CLASS ACT ★

by Kelly Starling Lyons
illustrated by Vanessa Brantley Newton

Penguin Workshop
An Imprint of Penguin Random House

PENGUIN WORKSHOP
Penguin Young Readers Group
An Imprint of Penguin Random House LLC

Penguin supports copyright. Copyright fuels creativity, encourages diverse voices, promotes free speech, and creates a vibrant culture. Thank you for buying an authorized edition of this book and for complying with copyright laws by not reproducing, scanning, or distributing any part of it in any form without permission. You are supporting writers and allowing Penguin to continue to publish books for every reader.

Text copyright © 2017 by Kelly Starling Lyons. Illustrations copyright © 2017 by Vanessa Brantley Newton. All rights reserved. Published by Penguin Workshop, an imprint of Penguin Random House LLC, 345 Hudson Street, New York, New York 10014. PENGUIN and PENGUIN WORKSHOP are trademarks of Penguin Books Ltd, and the W colophon is a trademark of Penguin Random House LLC. Manufactured in China.

Book design by Kayla Wasil.

Library of Congress Cataloging-in-Publication Data is available.

ISBN 9780451534279 (paperback)   10 9 8 7 6 5 4 3 2 1
ISBN 9780451534286 (library binding)   10 9 8 7 6 5 4 3 2 1

For the kids who dare to be
brave—and inspire me to do
the same—KSL
For every little girl in the
world, love—VBN

Chapter One: FRIENDLY COMPETITION

After the Pledge of Allegiance and announcements, Miss Taylor hit a silver chime with a small mallet. *Chirrr!* A high-pitched tone rang through our classroom. We hustled from our desks to sit in a circle on the orange-and-blue carpet. It was time for our morning meeting.

"Today is your chance to make a difference," Miss Taylor belted like a singer on TV. As she stretched out her arms, her bangles tinkled in harmony. We cheered for her performance.

"Do I have your attention?" she asked, beaming.

We smiled and nodded.

"Good. I have wonderful news: It's time to nominate a buddy or yourself to run for student council!"

Giggles and whispers rippled like a wave, spreading from one student to the next. Lena nudged my arm. Simone smiled and pointed at me across the circle.

I grinned, and my heart beat a little faster. Representing your class was a big deal. You got to come up with ideas to make the school better. You got to help plan events. You made sure your class had a voice. I wanted to run. But could I do it? I grabbed one of my braids and twisted it back and forth, back and forth around my finger as I thought it over.

"Class, class!" Miss Taylor called.

"Yes, yes." Instantly everyone quieted.

"I know you're excited," she said. "Let's talk about the qualities we'd like our student council representative to have."

Carson raised his hand first.

"Someone fair," he said.

"Somebody who knows what our class likes," Gabi offered.

I raised my hand.

"Someone who works hard and cares."

"Great list," Miss Taylor said. "We also want someone who can keep up with their schoolwork and student council responsibilities, like meeting after school, pitching in on projects, being a leader, and showing Brookside pride. Who can tell me what that means?"

"Positivity, respect, integrity, drive, and excellence," we all answered together.

"That's right," she said, smiling. "Being on student council is a lot of hard work, but it's a special honor. Okay, do we have any nomin—"

"Jada!" Simone hollered before she even finished.

My classmates clapped, and Lena hugged me around my shoulders.

"Miles!" RJ shouted. He was one of Miles's best friends and always had his back.

I applauded with the others as

Miles high-fived and fist-bumped
the kids sitting next to him. We were
always the top two in science—our
favorite subject. It would be fun
running for student council with him.
No matter what, we cheered each
other on.

"Anybody else?"

She looked around our circle,
pausing on each face. No takers.

"Jada and Miles, do you accept the nominations?"

We smiled at each other. My rainbow beads clacked and danced as I nodded.

"Okay, we have our candidates," Miss Taylor said, and handed each of us a blue paper that we and our parents had to sign. "This pledge has all of the guidelines. No put-downs.

No promises you can't keep. You have to make a poster with your campaign slogan and show respect to everyone who's running. And this year, we're doing something new. All of the fourth-grade candidates will get to give their speeches in the auditorium."

In the auditorium? I wrapped my braid around my finger and unwound it, twirled it and untwirled it, over and over.

"It will be great practice for fifth grade, when you can run for an office like president or vice president. That's when you can represent not just your class, but the whole school."

I couldn't even focus on the rest

of what Miss Taylor said. I'd have
no problem making the poster, but
giving a speech to the whole fourth
grade? Talk about torture. I sighed
and curled my braid around my
finger again. What had I gotten
myself into?

Chapter Two: Big Dreams, Big Doubts

A t home, I did my math worksheet and journal prompt, and then it was time to read with my little brother, Jackson. We had so many books in our family room, it looked like the library where Mom worked. It was one of the coolest places in our house.

Cozy reading nooks waited for someone to curl up in them. You could plop on Kente cloth beanbags, stretch out in the window seat, or snuggle into fluffy pillows on the comfy red couch. Picture books, chapter books, and novels packed the shelves. The fantasy and science fiction ones were my favorites. I loved exploring new worlds.

With Mom being a children's librarian, reading was like eating around here. Mom called books "food for our minds." But some days, Jax acted like reading a new book was as awful as someone asking him to take a bite of the vegetable he dreaded most—cauliflower. If the story wasn't about superheroes, vehicles, or Star Wars, he didn't want to try it. Even if he had to for homework.

"Are you ready to go on a ride?" I asked as we stood in front of the wall of bookshelves.

"Where are we going?" Jax replied, ready to pout.

"Let's fly to Hawaii today," I said, showing him a picture book about former president Barack Obama. I sank into the soft couch cushions and patted a spot next to me.

"Okay, Jax," I commanded. "Buckle up."

I snapped an imaginary seat belt in place. Then I waited for him to do the same. He looked like he wasn't sure if he wanted to get on board. "The pilot said we can't leave until you're safe."

"Pilot?" he asked.

Jax scrambled next to me, smiled, and pretended to fasten himself in.

"Click," he shouted.

"Get ready for takeoff in three . . . two . . . one. *Whoosh!*"

I opened the book, and we soared into the story. As we took turns reading about President Obama's life,

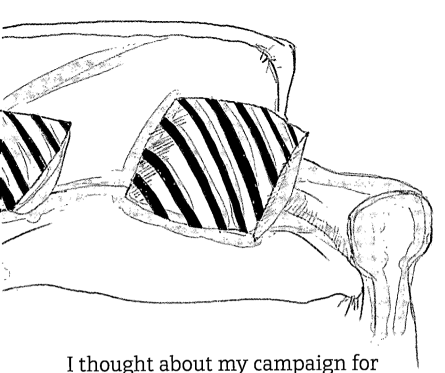

I thought about my campaign for
student council. I wanted to make a
difference and bring people together
too, but how could I do that when the
thought of talking to a crowd made
me want to hide?

After hanging out with Jax, I told
Mom the big news.

"Simone and Lena nominated me

for student council," I said. "Can you sign the paper saying it's okay for me to run?"

"Way to go, Jada!" Mom said. "Of course! Let me know if you want to talk about ideas. You know Dad and I have campaigned before. We can help."

Mom was vice president of her sorority. Dad was treasurer of his fraternity. They made running seem so easy. Why did it feel so hard? I wanted to be on student council, but I wondered if I should tell Miss Taylor I had changed my mind. When I was nervous about class presentations, I could take a breath, hold my hands to keep them still, and get through it. But the student council speech was in front of the whole fourth grade. Just thinking about it made me feel sick.

I remember the time I tried out for the Black History Month play. I wanted the part of astronaut Mae Jemison more than anything. I knew the lines. I could say them loud and with pride. But at tryouts, it felt like someone shook a Scrabble bag in my head, and I had to try to find the letters to spell each word before I said it. Finally, a line squeaked out. Mr. King, the music teacher, kept telling me to speak louder. I ended up as part of the chorus.

At dinner, Mom spilled the beans to Daddy.

"Jada is running for student council."

"Student council today. President tomorrow," he proudly announced.

"Like Barack Obama?" Jax asked.

I shook my head and tried to smile.

"You never know where things can lead," Mom said with a wink.

I knew everybody meant well, but all that talk about President Obama made worries start jumping

around in my head like popcorn in a microwave. I wasn't a great speaker like him, or even some of the kids my age. What if I froze up when it was my turn?

"Can I be excused?"

"Sure," Mom said. "Feeling okay?"

I nodded.

"Just want to work on my campaign."

In my room, I flopped on my daybed, squeezing my stuffed dragon, Steamy, and looked at my wall of heroes. There was Dr. Mae Jemison, along with Team USA's gold medal–winning women's gymnastics team, scientist Dr. George Washington Carver, and others I admired. They

faced challenges I couldn't even
imagine, but they believed in their
dreams. They sacrificed and worked
hard.

I heard a couple of raps on my
door, and then it opened.

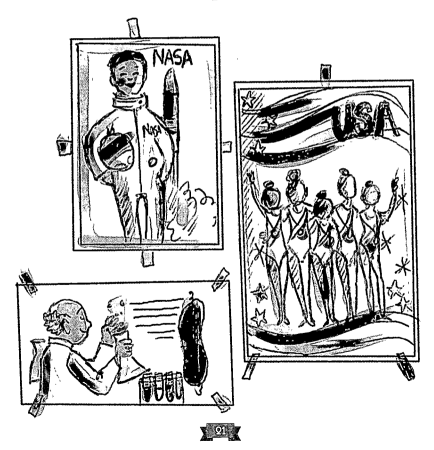

"How's it going?" Daddy asked, standing in my doorway. "Need any help with your campaign?"

"I don't know, Daddy," I said, and sighed. "I want to try for student council, but then I'm not so sure. I mean, I have to give a speech in front of everyone. I don't know if I can do it."

He walked in and sat on the edge of my bed.

"Well, your pop pop used to tell me, 'If you're going to let something hold you back, maybe you don't want it as badly as you think.' You don't have to run for student council. It's your decision. But if you do, go all in. You might surprise yourself."

Daddy hugged me and left me alone with my thoughts. Why did it feel like all of my heroes were staring at me, waiting for me to make the right choice?

I sat at my desk, opened a notebook, and grabbed my four-in-one pen. It was set to my best friend Mari's and my favorite color, purple.

When Mari moved away, I didn't think I'd ever be as close to someone as I was to her. Then I got to know Lena and Simone. Now, I had three besties. What if my campaign focused on being a friend? Running for student council wasn't about me. It was about helping the school, helping my classmates.

I looked at my heroes. If they could overcome challenges, I could, too. Did I want to be on student council? Yes!

I started writing down slogans. Then, one came to me that felt just right: "Vote for Jada: The Voice of a Friend."

Chapter Three:
TAKING SIDES

At lunch the next day, RJ jumped right into election talk.

"When you're on student council, Miles, can you get us more pizza days in the cafeteria?"

Everyone laughed.

"Who said I'm gonna win?" Miles said. "Jada could take it."

"I don't know," RJ said, frowning. "The kickball team is pretty big.

We'll vote for you. Right, everyone?"

Kyla and the rest of their crew nodded and gave thumbs-up.

While RJ talked, Simone rolled her eyes. Finally, she couldn't hold it in any longer.

"Are you serious?" she asked. "Jada has the jump rope vote. And the science club."

"Miles is in science club, too," RJ countered.

My stomach lurched as Simone and RJ squabbled back and forth, trying to make their case. Miles and I both wanted to help the school. I'd love to be on student council, but why did it have to pit us against each other?

As the bickering grew louder, the lunch monitor frowned and slid a red plastic cup on top of the green one in the middle of our table. That meant no more talking.

Miles and I looked at each other and shook our heads. As we lined up to go to recess, Miles whispered, "Good luck, Jada."

Before I could wish the same to him, RJ cut between us. I sighed and didn't bother calling him out.

Our friends were out of control. But that was their problem, not ours. On the playground, Simone and Lena sat with me under the shade of the big leafy tree.

"So what's our plan to beat Miles?" Simone asked.

I grimaced and shook my head.

"Miles is cool," I said. "It's not about beating him. I just want to do my best."

"You do that, and we'll work on the winning part," Simone said, grinning. Her tapping feet made her shimmering sneakers flash.

"It's so awesome you're running," Lena said.

"I'm excited, but I wish I didn't have to talk in front of everyone. You were at the play tryouts. Remember what happened? I was like a statue and could barely move my mouth. Speeches just aren't my thing."

I heard a twig crack and jumped. Oh no! Was someone listening? I didn't want everyone knowing my big fear. I looked around and didn't see anyone but us. I inhaled and tried to stop freaking out.

"Don't worry. You'll be awesome," Lena said. "The play was last year."

She always knew what to say.

"Yeah, you can practice on Lena and me," Simone said. "Miss Taylor says I have the gift of gab. I can give you tips on speaking to a group."

I smiled. Simone was a fantastic speaker.

"And I can help you with polishing the speech," Lena said. I loved being partnered with her when we did writing workshops in class. She gave great comments and wanted to be an author when she grew up.

I started feeling better, like maybe with my friends behind me, I could face anything.

"Yeah, we can definitely help you,"
Simone said. "Then, you can help us."

Uh-oh. Just like that, I got a queasy
feeling in my stomach.

"Student council means you can
get things our class wants, right? How
about more recess? We never have
enough time. What do you think we
need, Lena?"

"More field trips would be amazing. We only went to the art museum in third grade."

I reached for a braid and twirled it around my finger. Didn't the pledge say no making promises you can't keep?

"I don't know," I said cautiously.

Simone and Lena got called to jump, their favorite activity.

"Wanna come?"

"I'll be over in a little while," I said.

Maybe I wasn't right for student council. Not only did I have to give a big speech, I had to let down my BFFs. I picked up some rocks and studied them, wishing they held the answer to my problems.

"Find anything?" Miles asked.

"Not really looking," I said. "Just hanging out. Did you start working on your poster?"

"A little," he said. "How about you? I know it's gonna be good."

I smiled. But before I could answer, there was RJ again. He barely looked at me.

"Why are you talking to *her*?" he said to Miles, spitting out "her" so it sounded like an insult. "We need you in the game. You're up in a minute."

"See ya, Jada," Miles called.

Why did it feel like it would be a long time before we really talked? Did running for student council mean losing a friend?

Chapter Four:
RUMOR SQUAD

Simone and Lena came over to my house after school to help me work on my campaign. I showed them what I had so far—a poster with "Vote for Jada" in violet block letters at the top and "The Voice of a Friend" underneath.

"I love that," Lena said. "You're definitely a great friend."

"Looks good," Simone said.

"But it could use some sparkle so it really stands out."

Above my slogan, I drew a picture of a girl in the middle holding hands with kids on each side. There were tall kids and short ones, girls and boys. Some had glasses or freckles. Their skin colors spanned from peach to chocolate. I wanted to be someone who was there for everyone.

The next day, I taped up my poster in the classroom. Miles hung up his too. In gold letters it said: "Want someone who goes the extra mile? Vote for Miles." It shined above a black road leading to a yellow sign that said "Success."

"Cool slogan," I told him.

"Yours is great, too."

"Wonderful job," Miss Taylor said, admiring our posters with our classmates. "How are your speeches coming along?"

"Okay," I said slowly. I wondered if I should tell her I was nervous. Would she understand?

"Almost there," Miles said, grinning.

Figured. Miles always did great at presentations. I decided to keep my worries to myself. I would find a way to make it work.

"I'm proud of both of you. I can't wait to hear you share."

At lunch, RJ sat next to me. He tapped my shoulder.

"Cool poster," he said. "But I have a question."

"What?"

"How are you going to be the voice of our class when you're scared to talk?"

I could hear my heart thumping in my ears. But I stared him down and tried to keep my voice steady.

"Whatever, RJ," I said.

He moved down a few seats to sit with the kickball crew. Whatever he said made everyone look at me and laugh.

I tried to act like I didn't care. But his words were all I could think about. I looked around for Miles. He was still in the lunch line. I wound a braid around my finger. How did RJ know my big fear? When I got up to dump my lunch tray, I passed RJ and his crew.

"Did you say something, Jada?" he asked as I walked by.

"No."

"I didn't think so. Talking isn't your thing, right?"

His friends giggled, while Miles frowned after sitting at the table.

"Quit it, RJ!" Miles said.

As soon as I got time with Simone and Lena at recess, I started questioning them.

"Did you tell anybody I was nervous about giving the speech?"

"What? I wouldn't do that," Lena said. "Cross my heart."

"Simone?"

"No way!"

"Then how did RJ find out?"

I couldn't believe that the one thing I wanted to keep quiet was the talk of lunch. We tried to figure out how RJ had heard. Suddenly Simone scrunched her eyebrows together and got a lightbulb look, like the answer just came to her. A second later, her face drooped.

"I think I saw someone walking by when we were talking," she said slowly.

"Was it RJ?" I asked, ready to let him have it.

"No," she said, looking down.

"Who was it?"

Simone looked up, and our eyes met.

"I think it was Miles."

My heart sank. Miles? I remembered hearing that cracking twig and feeling panicked as I looked around. But I didn't see anyone. And there's no way Miles would say something to make me look bad.

"You must be mixed-up. He would never spread a rumor about me," I said, trying to put my mind on something else. "Let's jump."

Lena and Simone were two of the best double Dutchers in our school and promised to give me some tips.

"Watch the ropes for your chance to jump in," Lena said.

I rocked back and forth as the ropes twirled, trying to get the rhythm. After a few tries, I made it.

The pitter-patter of my feet and the clicking of my bouncing beads made me forget all about the RJ drama. Then, next thing I knew, there he was.

"Jada, you don't really want to run for student council, do you?

You'd have to stand in front of the whole auditorium. Think of all those people staring at you."

"Leave her alone, RJ," Lena said. "She's trying to jump."

"You just worry about Miles, RJ," Simone fired back while she turned. "Jada will be just fine."

"That's not what I heard," RJ said. "Miles said Jada froze up at the play tryouts."

I couldn't hear anything else. Not the beat of the rope. Not the click of my beads or the chirps of the birds flying overhead. Not the laughs of my classmates having fun. Just what RJ said Miles told him. I looked down. The ropes were tangled around my feet.

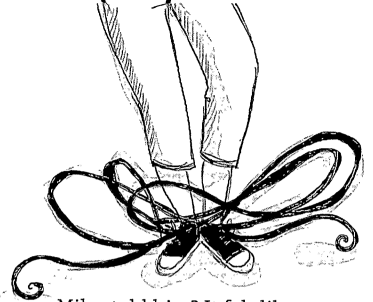

Miles told him? It felt like my heart was a glass that fell to the pavement and smashed into a million pieces. I thought Miles was cool. I thought he was my friend. I didn't believe it.

"You made that up, RJ," I shot at him.

"Ask him yourself," he said, and walked away.

"Sorry, Jada," Lena whispered.

I glared at Miles across the playground. When he smiled at me, I frowned. Forget about rooting for each other. This meant war.

Chapter Five: FRENEMIES

Every time I saw Miles, I looked the other way. I couldn't believe he would start a rumor about me. But RJ said Miles told him. He even dared me to ask him. How else would he find out? It seemed like everyone was talking about the big freeze at the tryouts and wondering if I was going to turn icicle again. Kids would whisper when I came near and then stop and whisper again when I walked by.

At lunch, Miles and I usually sat next to each other, or just with a couple of kids between us. But now . . . I looked down at the opposite end of the table and saw Miles next to RJ. We might as well have been on different planets. Simone, Lena, Carson, and other jumpers lumped together on my side.

RJ, Kyla, and the rest of the kickball crew clustered around Miles. The chorus kids and the science clubbers sat in between.

At recess, Miles and I avoided each other. Then he came to the side of the playground where we jumped, near the monkey bars and slide.

"I'm sorry, Jada," he said. "I didn't mean to tell RJ. I was just—"

"Whatever." I turned and pretended like I didn't hear him

talking after that. I didn't like treating Miles that way, but he hurt me.

"Maybe you should listen to him," Lena said as he walked away. "He seems pretty sad."

I saw Miles leaning against the fence with his head down. I felt bad but thought about how much RJ's nasty words stung and looked away.

But one thing RJ's actions did was give me motivation. Knowing he wanted me to fall apart made me determined to do my best. I practiced my speech with Mom and Dad. I said it for Jax and his Star Wars action figures. I read it in front of Simone and Lena when they came over during the weekend.

"That was good," Simone said, leaning on a beanbag. "Talk slower and louder next time. Keep your head up. If you get nervous, breathe. And don't forget to tell everyone you'll get us more recess and field trips. That will get you votes for sure."

My stomach flip-flopped as I thought about the pledge. I couldn't guarantee those things. But Simone and Lena helped me. What if they were mad at me for not including what they wanted? I already lost Miles as a friend. I couldn't lose them, too.

I sighed and took a breath.

"What's wrong, Jada?" Lena asked.

Maybe I should just make the promises. Breaking the pledge would take me out of the running for student council. Maybe everything would go back to normal, and Miles and I would return to being friends. But I really wanted to make a difference. Or at least try. I inhaled again.

"I can't say that."

"Why not?" Simone said.

"Miss Taylor said we can't make promises we can't keep. If I make student council, I can share what our class wants. But I'm not going to say I can deliver."

"Okay," Simone said.

"Okay?"

"Yep. We're BFFs, right?"

"Yes!"

All of that worry for nothing. It just took me being honest to clear it up. I felt like I could float around the room. If only it was that easy to deal with Miles and his crew.

Chapter Six:
GAME OVER

The next morning, I noticed Miles walking around the classroom searching for something. He looked in his backpack and cubby, through the bins near Miss Taylor's desk, on the floor.

"He can't find his math homework," Lena whispered. "You know what happens if he doesn't turn it in on time."

No homework meant you missed
out on part of recess. I felt bad as I
watched RJ help him look. Any other
day, I would help, too. But I thought
about what Miles did to me and
headed for the reading corner. As I
searched for a new novel, I pulled
out a book with a paper peeking out.

I unfolded the paper and couldn't believe it. Miles's homework! I glanced over my shoulder. Miles was slumped at his desk with his head in his hand. I knew I should tell him right away that I'd found it. But I thought about the rumor, and before I knew it, I was back at my desk.

I kept staring at the homework

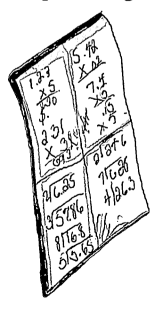

and then at Miles. His bottom lip stuck out. He looked just miserable. I couldn't let him get in trouble. I had

to tell Miles about the homework
soon, but I told myself to wait. After
what he did to me, he deserved to
worry a little.

Chirr!

Meeting time. On the carpet, some
kids scooted away from each other.
Some whispered and glared. Miss
Taylor looked at us with her I've-had-
enough face.

"Class, class!" she called.

"Yes, yes."

"Someone tell me what's going on.
Now!"

"Miles started a rumor about
Jada being scared to talk in the
auditorium," Simone blurted out all in
a rush.

Miss Taylor's face tightened. She turned to Miles and frowned.

"Is that true, Miles?" she asked. "Did you tell your friends that Jada was afraid to present?"

It was so quiet we could hear every breath, every fidget, as we waited for Miles to answer. He bit his bottom lip, and his eyes blurred like he was about to cry.

"I didn't mean to," he said slowly. "It slipped out."

"Miles Lewis, I'm surprised and disappointed. You signed a pledge about no put-downs. I'm going to have to tell your parents and disqualify you from running for student council. Jada will be our class representative."

Just like that, I got student council, and Miles got a consequence. But as I looked at Miles with his teary eyes, I didn't feel like celebrating. My throat felt full. I wanted to cry, too.

"And for each person who told someone else that rumor, how would you feel if someone shared a secret about you? You have a choice: You can spread gossip or you can spread goodwill."

Around the circle, everyone bowed their heads and stared at the floor. This wasn't how I wanted to win. My campaign was called "The Voice of a Friend," and I wasn't acting like one. I thought about Miles's homework sitting on my desk and how sad he looked. Why didn't I give it to him right away? If Miles didn't deserve to be on student council, I didn't either.

I stopped twisting my braid, gulped, and raised my hand.

"Yes, Jada?" Miss Taylor said.

"I . . . I . . . I didn't keep my pledge either," I admitted. "When I found out that Miles overheard me and told RJ, I was mean and didn't even give him a chance to explain. I even did something today to get back at him."

I stood, walked over to my desk, and picked up the math paper. I handed it to Miles.

"Here's your homework," I said. "I saw it when I went to get a new book. It was folded up inside. I wasn't going to let you get in trouble, but I let you worry, even though I had it. That was wrong."

I turned to Miss Taylor.

"Someone else should be on student council."

Lena put her arm around my shoulder when I sat back in my spot.

"I see," Miss Taylor said, looking at every face in the circle. "I'm sure you and

Miles weren't the only ones behaving badly. Sounds like it has been going around."

The silence was painful, like when you're in trouble with your parents but don't know what to say. RJ looked at Miles, at me, then at the floor. Then back to Miles and me. Slowly he raised his hand.

"RJ?"

"Miles didn't start a rumor about Jada," he said, looking down. "It was me. Miles overheard Jada sharing what happened at the play tryouts last year and said it wasn't fair that she had to speak onstage. He said just because you give a great speech doesn't mean you're the best

for student council. It was me who started spreading things around. Sorry."

One after another, classmates chimed in, sharing how they were part of the problem. Some said they sat away from others and snubbed them. Others revealed that they made a promise to vote for Miles or me not because of our campaigns, but because we were their friends.

"We all messed up," Simone said. "But Miles and Jada are awesome. Can they please have another chance?"

She pressed her hands together.

"Please?" the class joined in.

Miss Taylor looked like she was thinking it over.

"I think you all deserve another chance," she said finally. "Speaking up is tough. The class will get a consequence: silent lunch. RJ, you'll have an additional one: walking laps at recess. Then, we'll start over fresh."

She smiled at us. "I'm proud of you for doing what's right."

Then she turned to me.

"Jada, if you're still feeling nervous, how about we let you and Miles just present to our class?"

A way out! I exhaled, slow and long. It felt good to be off the hook. Then I thought about my mom and dad, my heroes, my class. If I was going to stand up for others, then I had to face my fear.

"No, I want to do it," I heard myself say.

And I meant it. Even if I froze. Even if I couldn't find the words. Even if I trembled onstage and wanted to hide, I would try.

Chapter Seven:
SHOW TIME

Now that Miles and I were back in the running, he came up with an idea to help both of us. We could give our speeches the day before the assembly to just our class for practice. Miss Taylor loved it.

On the day of our trial run, Miles volunteered to go first. He stood up straight and spoke with expression. He looked at everyone in the class

and made you feel like he was talking
to you.

"I'll put in the work. I'll go the
extra mile. If you believe I can help
our class and our school, vote for
Miles."

Everyone cheered. Then, it was my
turn. As I stood in front of the class,
my hands fidgeted. My paper rustled.
I looked at the words and breathed in
and out.

"You got it, Jada," Miles called.

I looked up and saw a room of
smiling faces. Then the shiny purple
banner over Miss Taylor's door caught
my eye, "Believe." I saw it every day,
but today it meant something special.
I started to read.

BELIEVE

"When my best friend Mari moved away," I said, "I didn't think I'd ever make another friend. But I forgot that I had a whole class of them."

I looked around the room.

"You laughed at my jokes. You cheered me on. You taught me what being a friend means. Now I want to give something back to you. I want to give something back to our school. I'll work hard, make sure to listen, and speak up when I need to. If you choose me, I'll be the voice of a friend, someone you can count on."

The booming claps made me feel like dancing. I didn't care if I won the class election. I was already a winner.

Chapter Eight: Winning Combination

For the big day, I dressed up in a bright lavender shirt with a colorful scarf and my favorite patterned pants. Mom told me I looked bold and confident. I hoped I would feel that way, too.

Miles, the other candidates, and I sat on the side of the stage. One by one, each class shared their speeches. Then ours was up. Miles did amazing.

I saw kids smiling as he spoke. Teachers nodded. The thundering applause shook the room.

"Jada Jones for Miss Taylor's class," the assistant principal, Mrs. Keane, announced as I walked to center stage.

My hands quivered. I laid my speech on the lectern and gazed at the staring faces. My brain started to jumble. My heart pounded. I kept my eyes on my paper.

"Start when you're ready," Mrs. Keane whispered to me.

I breathed in and out. All I had to do was read. I pictured Mom, Dad, and Jax cheering me on. I thought about the "Believe" banner above

Miss Taylor's door. I looked up and focused on my class. You can do it, I told myself over and over.

I read my speech slowly at first, softly and carefully saying each word. But as I got going, something happened. My hands stilled. My voice rose clear and strong. I knew I didn't

need the paper anymore. I looked out at my friends and spoke from my heart.

When I finished, cheers rocked the auditorium.

"Thank you, Jada," Mrs. Keane said.

I glided back to my seat. I did it!

"That was awesome," Miles said when I sat next to him.

Back in our classroom, Miss Taylor passed out ballots.

"I am proud of both of our candidates," she said, smiling at each of us. "And everyone in this room. Both Miles and Jada would be excellent picks to represent our class. The choice is up to you."

We put up our privacy screens and voted. Miss Taylor said she would announce the results at our morning meeting.

The next day, it felt like the announcements would never end. Finally, Miss Taylor stood up and hit the chime. *Chirr!* We scrambled into a circle.

"I am pleased to say we have a

student council representative," she said. "Drumroll, please."

We used our hands like drumsticks and beat out a rumbling sound on our legs.

"Jada Jones!"

Did Miss Taylor say my name? I couldn't believe it. Before I knew it, everyone was congratulating me.

"Way to go, Jada," Kyla hollered.

"Jada! Jada!" Simone kicked off a chant that spread around the circle.

"Class, class!" Miss Taylor called.

"Yes, yes."

"Let's hear it for Miles! He'll be our alternate, and did a great job."

We whooped and stood up to cheer. I gave my friend a thumbs-up.

On the way back to my desk, I noticed RJ standing next to my chair. I wondered what he wanted.

"Congratulations, Jada," he said, grinning. I took my seat and couldn't stop smiling.

I couldn't wait until Mom and Dad heard I made student council. If I could do this, I could do anything.

JADA'S RULES FOR BEING A CLASS ACT

1. Believe in yourself.

2. Say no to drama.

3. Speak up, even if it's hard.

4. Try to fix your mistakes.

5. Be a friend.

ACKNOWLEDGMENTS

Thank you to the rock stars of Penguin Workshop, my amazing agent Caryn Wiseman, and brilliant illustrator and sister-friend Vanessa Brantley Newton. I'm so grateful for all of the people who offered encouragement and support on this book. Special shout-outs to: Patrick, Jordan and Josh Lyons, Deborah Starling, Delores Walker, Don Tate, Dr. Pauletta Brown Bracy, Judy Allen Dodson, Susan Stewart Taylor, and Shelia Reich.